"Adventurous, funny, sometimes terrifying; you haven't lived until you've read this book, so if you want to live, read it."

Ciera Fiaschetti, age 10

"If you don't read this book you will and I quote get payback."

Amy Cook, age 10

"Warning: 99% chance of death. This book might make you cry."

Cody Curran, age 11

"Step in this book if you dare, but you better beware of what's inside here."

Gabe Frankel, age 10

CHECK OUT CHOOSE YOUR OWN NIGHTMARES:
EIGHTH GRADE WITCH
BLOOD ISLAND

YOU MIGHT ALSO ENJOY THESE BESTSELLERS...

CHOOSE YOUR OWN ADVENTURE®

THE ABOMINABLE SNOWMAN

JOURNEY UNDER THE SEA

SPACE AND BEYOND

THE LOST JEWELS
OF NABOOTI

MYSTERY OF THE MAYA

HOUSE OF DANGER

RACE FOREVER

ESCAPE

LOST ON THE AMAZON

PRISONER OF THE
ANT PEOPLE

TROUBLE ON PLANET EARTH

WAR WITH THE EVIL
POWER MASTER

CUP OF DEATH

THE CASE OF THE SILK KING

BEYOND ESCAPE!

SECRET OF THE NINJA

THE BRILLIANT DR. WOGAN

RETURN TO ATLANTIS

FORECAST FROM
STONEHENGE

INCA GOLD

STRUGGLE DOWN UNDER

TATTOO OF DEATH

SILVER WINGS

TERROR ON THE TITANIC

SEARCH FOR THE
MOUNTAIN GORILLAS

MOON QUEST

PROJECT UFO

ISLAND OF TIME

SMOKE JUMPERS

CHINESE DRAGONS

TRACK STAR!

U.N. ADVENTURE:
MISSION TO MOLOWA

BLOOD ON THE HANDLE

ZOMBIE PENPAL

BEHIND THE WHEEL

PUNISHMENT: EARTH

PIRATE TREASURE OF THE
ONYX DRAGON

SEARCH FOR THE
BLACK RHINO

THE CURSE OF THE
PIRATE MIST

TRAIL OF LOST TIME

BY BALLOON TO
THE SAHARA

ESCAPE FROM THE
HAUNTED WAREHOUSE

WAREHOUSE

BY ANSON MONTGOMERY

ILLUSTRATED BY KEITH NEWTON

CHOOSECO
WAITSFIELD, VERMONT

Illustrated by: Keith Newton
Book design: Stacey Boyd, Big Eyedea Visual Design

For information regarding permission, write to:

CHOOSECO

P.O. Box 46
Waitsfield, Vermont 05673
www.cyoa.com

ISBN-13: 978-1-937133-47-4
ISBN-10: 1-937133-47-8

Published simultaneously in the United States and Canada

Printed in Canada

10 9 8 7 6 5 4 3 2 1

*This is book is dedicated to my father,
R. A. Montgomery. He taught me so many
things about life. How to explore mountains,
cherish your friends, love your family, find new
adventures and to have a fresh view on the
many wonders of the world while always seeing
the humor in life. Thank you, Dad!*

BEWARE and WARNING!

This book is different from other books. You and YOU ALONE are in charge of what happens in this story.

There are dangers, choices, adventures, and consequences. YOU must use all of your talents and intelligence to determine how the story ends. The wrong decision could end in disaster—even DEATH! But don't despair. At any time, YOU can go back and make another choice, alter the path of your story, and change its result.

It all starts when you need a summer job to buy textbooks and put gas in your car. So you answer a mysterious ad for the graveyard shift at a spooky warehouse. Del Grady gives you the job on the spot. He tells you that the warehouse stores movie props and aisle after aisle of boring boxes filled with boring stuff. Or does it? Your solo nighttime hours mean whole shifts spent alone in this eerie place. Grady can't seem to keep everything under control, and you must battle a long-dead countess who wants your head, a bloodthirsty wolfhound, and a sharp-shooting team of ghost hunters who work for the FBI. You signed up for a paycheck, but will you live to see another summer?

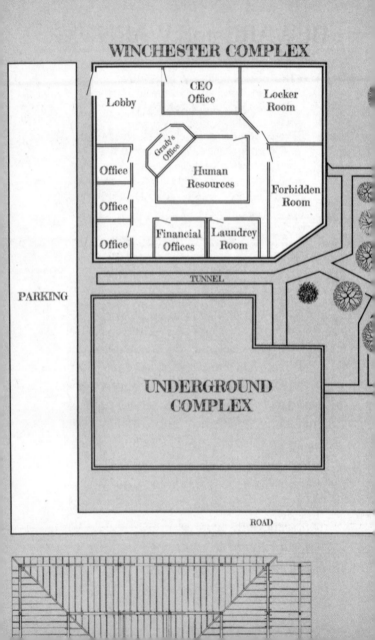

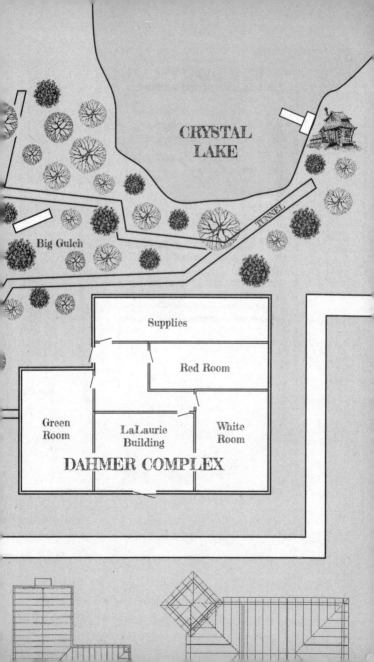

SUPER SUMMER
JOB OPENING!!

Are you exceptional? A self-starter? Able to work on your own? Open to working the 'graveyard' shift? Not bothered or scared by working in the darkness of deep night? If the answer is to all of the above is 'YES!', then apply for our new Warehouse Intern position! Tired of the cut-throat, rat-race real world? Spend your summer preparing for magical, mystical and mysterious productions! Competitive wages! Frequent light and occasional heavy lifting required. Apply in person at our facility at 999 Kiln Road (2 blocks past the old crematory). No calls. Mon-Weds. 11 PM–3:30 AM EEOE. All beings welcome to apply! No background check! POSITION MUST BE FILLED!!! APPLY TONIGHT!!!

As strange as the ad was, you are desperate enough to find a job that you decide to take a chance. Your gas tank is running empty and the night is dark as you drive past the old crematory on the edge of town. Pulling up to the huge, hulking form of the mostly dark warehouse, you feel a twinge of fear. *Why am I in the middle of nowhere at midnight?* you ask yourself, but you enter the strange building complex anyway.

There is no one in the front room, but there is a neatly hand-lettered sign that says: "Warehouse Interned Applicants This Way →." You follow the sign and knock on the open doorway of a small, old-fashioned office. Stacks of paper and a corded telephone are the only things on the desk except for the nameplate: "Warehouse Manager: Mr. Del Grady." A man is writing on a sheet of paper. He is slight, oldish, and deeply pale. He wears a striped suit and a skinny tie.

"Come in, you're late," he says without looking up.

"Uh, I don't think so," you reply.

He looks up at you and gives a short laugh. "Hah! You're late for the graveyard shift! It's 12:01, after the witching hour!"

You nod in response, not knowing what else to do.

Turn to the next page.

"You'll be moving items, boxed up, from place to place in the building," Mr. Grady explains as he shows you around the huge, darkened warehouse. "You'll be busy!" he adds with a sharp laugh. "There's lots to move!"

"We aren't shipping out from the warehouse, just moving around inside of it? Why?" you ask as you follow him into a cavernous storage area with metal shelves rising far above your head into the deep darkness and far off into the distance.

"Well...yes, of course, we do ship things. Sometimes. You see," Mr. Grady says with a long pause before continuing, "...certain items need to be in certain places at specific times. We are a very specialized storage and delivery warehouse. We send things to...movies. Hollywood, you know, props, scenery, that kind of stuff," he explains. "Ah! Here we are," he says as you reach a red door with the words Employees Only! stenciled in white. "This is your locker room where you'll change into your work uniform."

"Um, Mr. Grady, I'm not sure I've actually accepted the job yet? I haven't even filled out the application," you say.

"Is that so?" he says, turning to face you in the weak red light from the caged emergency bulb above the door. "It feels like you're already part of the family! Anyway, you'll be perfect," he says, opening the door to the locker room.

Turn to page 4.

4

As you navigate through the dark warehouse several days later, you wonder: *Why did I take this job?* You needed the money for tuition, not to mention books, school supplies, gas, and food! After your weird interview, you scrambled to find something else, anything else. A job at the pizza parlor fell through and your uncle Charlie couldn't afford to bring you on to his landscaping company because work had slowed down for his crew.

You are a true night owl now, spending your days sleeping and your overnights in dark hallways, pushing thousands of pounds of boxes and crates from storage room to storage room.

Go on to the next page.

From the day you had your interview until now, everything seemed mysterious. The only cool thing is the powered hand lift that you use to move all the stuff from place to place. The Model B-200 Powered Hand Truck with the stencil "B-WARE1 for Warehouse #1" on it is your only company most nights. Your assistant B-WARE1 helps you lift huge pallets and zip them around. Occasionally you find yourself talking to B-WARE1 as if it were a person. You use your hand to steady the load you've just scooped up. The boxes are too long to fit on the pallets neatly. Sweat starts to drip into your eyes and off the end of your nose. It has been a hot, humid summer, and you wish that this latest heat wave would break. "Hot tonight, B-WARE!" you say out loud.

Turn to the next page.

The dim, flickering lights that line the hallway give everything a spooky look, and you can't wipe your sweaty face because you need both hands to guide B-WARE when he's all loaded up. With all the mass on your buddy, it is hard to stop once it gets moving. The first few times you had to move a big load you would bang into the walls and go side to side like a bowling ball with kiddie bumpers in the gutters. But now you have gotten the hang of it. You know when to apply slight pressure to move the B-WARE in the right direction.

What's in these boxes? you wonder for probably the thousandth time this summer. No one has told you anything about what the warehouse holds. You have not learned much more about the company since Mr. Grady's explanation at your "interview," but at least they pay you well.

Mr. Grady scheduled you for the graveyard shift, from midnight until 8 AM, so that everything "would be in place for the next night." You've only seen Mr. Grady twice since. "I'll be in my office, down the main corridor, and my door is always open!" He must have meant that figuratively as every time you've passed by it has been shut with no light peeking out from under the door.

Go on to the next page.

The warehouse is a huge complex, with a vast underground network of tunnels connecting multiple buildings. You and B-WARE1 work alone, but sometimes you hear machinery running in the other buildings while you work: *BOOM-chunk-CRACK*. Occasionally you'll see dark shadows or silhouettes in the lit windows in other buildings, but you never see any other workers. Each night you go into the empty locker room to find a list (with helpful highlighted maps) of what you are supposed to move from location to location. Every spot in the warehouse is labeled with numbers and names. "Move Usher Crate 21 to Room 13 in the Winchester Complex," or "Take Borden Box 40 to Dragsholm Slot 12 in the LaLaurie Building." But there is never a description of what is inside.

Your reverie is broken by a scream, or howl, coming from the doorway directly to the left of the B-WARE.

OOOORROOWOOOOROOOOORRROOOR-RRR-yeeeeeeeeeeeeee!!!!

Turn to the next page.

The cart crashes into the wall, and the wooden pallet stacked with cardboard boxes crunches and breaks. You have to dive to keep the box from sliding off and hitting the floor.

The howl-scream stops for a second, but then it starts again. Is it a person, or an animal, crying in pain? You try the door, but it won't open. Unlike many of the other locked doors in the warehouse, this one does not have a padlock, and the door itself is a flimsy one with loose hinges. You might be able to break it down if you really tried. Or you could go get Mr. Grady. He has the keys to all of the rooms. What should you do? The scream starts up again. You have to do something!

If you try and break the door down, turn to page 20.

If you decide to get Mr. Grady and the key, turn to page 33.

You couldn't live with yourself if you did not at least try to unlock the secrets of the warehouse by meeting its mysterious owner.

"Odd choice," Mr. Grady says, "you may wish the countess had finished her job!" That laugh. It is only getting more annoying with repetition.

"Look, Grady, I'm tired and you promised answers. Make it quick or I'll just leave."

"I wish it were that simple," he replies, standing up. "Follow me."

Thinking you made the wrong choice, you stand up planning to walk out the door and just go home anyway, but you find yourself walking down the hallway with Mr. Grady. You feel like you are floating. Soon you are in an area that you have never been to before. Mr. Grady leads you down and down. The railing of the stairwell is wrought iron. It gets hot as you reach a landing and come into a furnace room. Piles of coal are heaped all about the gigantic room. Six different furnaces are going full bore. Men shovel coal into the flaming maws of the furnaces without stopping. The air is smoky and smells of burning coal. You come to a door that says: "Administrative Head: Mr. Tory Perga." Grady opens the door and you follow him inside.

Turn to page 11.

Inside the room, it is cool, sweet-smelling, and white. A black desk straight in front of you dominates the room with its darkness. You think it might be carved out of a single piece of black granite, onyx, obsidian, or maybe jet? A man in a well-fitted dark gray suit stands in front of the back wall which is displaying a variety of security camera views, spreadsheets, documents, and charts. His back is to you.

"Um, Mr. Perga," Mr. Grady says timidly after giving a slight cough. He seems nervous in front of his boss. "We're here. I mean, about the situation we had earlier tonight, with…the countesses. You know."

Turn to the next page.

12

"Indeed I do, Grady, indeed I do," replies the deep voice of Mr. Perga.

He waves his hand at the back wall and it transforms into a mirrored surface for an instant before turning into a long view of what you believe to be the Tuscan countryside. Olive groves, red-tiled villas and mountains dominate the view. It looks very real and you see trees swaying gently in the breeze. But for a moment, when the wall was a mirror, you locked eyes with Mr. Perga through the reflection. He had a dark beard, neatly cropped, with a handsome but remote face and a nose that cut down the middle of his face. His eyes were black, blacker even than Mr. Grady's. You did not like meeting his eyes. Your hands start to twitch.

"What happened tonight?" you ask, a little aggressively. You are still scared from the whole night so far. "Mr. Grady said that I'm not dreaming, but I think this has to be a dream. What is the warehouse? Why am I here?"

"The best way to answer those questions is to ask you one. What is your name?" Mr. Perga says, still keeping his back to you.

Go on to the next page.

A strange fog in your head prevents you from answering automatically, as you have so many times in the past. You struggle for a minute. "Well, my uncle Charlie couldn't give me enough work this summer with his landscaping business, so I started working for Mr. Grady…"

"I didn't ask you about your uncle Charlie. I asked your name. Some other questions to consider are these. How long have you been working here? Why is it always summer? Where do you live?"

You try to remember. It feels just out of reach.

Turn to the next page.

14

"I don't know," you finally respond. You feel empty, drained, and even more scared than before. Why can't you remember your own name? Maybe it is amnesia, like in a soap opera?

"We are the warehouse for those things that can't advance. You are relatively new. Only manifest for a few years," Mr. Perga explains. He clasps his hands behind his back. "Your murder in the storage warehouse was so traumatic that you became...stuck. It was a workplace rage thing, you barely knew him. He killed thirteen people before the police shot him."

"What do you mean, 'my murder'?" you ask, feeling the edge of a memory. A loud noise...then silence.

"We decided to integrate you into your present reality in a measured manner," Mr. Perga answers, not explaining. "Your work in the warehouse, staging the props for the performances, was intended to slowly give you the basis to understand your situation. Clearly that didn't happen, and for that I apologize. The countesses are more troublesome than all the other haunts combined. They enjoy tormenting those weaker than themselves."

Go on to the next page.

"But...that's not true! I'm not some stupid ghost!" you blurt, your heart racing in your chest.

"You're not stupid," Mr. Perga replies, "but you *are* a ghost." He turns towards you and there is a nothingness where his face should be. It hurts to look at it. "Feel the back of your head, then get back to work. We're behind schedule."

Numbly, you feel the back of your head. Your hand touches the sharp edges of the hole in your skull, feels the wetness of the soft matter within, and drops to your side. You wipe the blood on your pants, turn and get back to work.

The End

"Mr. Grady gave the key to me, and I don't think he'd like it if I gave it to strangers," you say. You don't trust Mr. Grady enough to know or care what he would think, but you need a reasonable excuse not to hand over the key to two people with drawn guns. A bead of sweat drops off the end of your nose.

"Do you know what Grady is?" the woman asks you before answering herself. "Of course not, otherwise you'd have done the right thing."

"Take the key," Johnson says in a flat voice.

"No, Agent Johnson, we're not going to rob this kid of the key right now, even if it would be the smart play and make our job easier," she says with a weary sigh, before turning to you. "Good luck with the key, kid. I hope that you make it out of this craziness. I hope that we all make it out of here!"

"Yeah, me too." you say as you turn to the door.

CRACK! A blazing pain spreads from the back of your skull.

Turn to the next page.

You fall to the floor, twitching.

"Listen, Andre! No need to hurt the kid!" the woman hisses.

"Not hurt. Sleeping," Johnson says.

CRACK!

You pass out from the pain.

You wake to someone gently shaking your shoulder. The pain in your head is still monstrous, but better than it was. You gingerly feel your head and your hand touches your still-sticky, blood-matted hair.

"You okay, kid?" the gray-haired woman asks you. She wears a badge that says "Winchester Mystery House, San Jose, CA: My Name is: Agatha." She looks nice, but worried.

"How'd you get in here? What happened to your head? Are you all right?" she asks.

"Not really," you manage. Your voice is hoarse and dry. You notice that you are in the room with the bed and two chairs. Bright daylight streams in through a window that wasn't there last night.

"Are we really in California?" you ask.

"Of course!" Agatha says, "Why wouldn't it be California?"

"I thought I was a long way from California. I've never been there."

Your head throbs.

"I think I need to see a doctor."

The End

You decide to play their stupid game. The woman from your dream, Ms. Garcia, was trying to help you! You meet with Mr. Akfak to set up an appointment with Hepburn and Padurii, and he gives you the usual run-around. Just as you're about to leave, you say, "May I have a Form: 9696, please, Mr. Akfak?"

He breaks into a little smile, opens a drawer in his desk, and hands you the form.

"Thank you!" you say, with more emotion in your voice than you intended.

"You had only to ask!"

The transfer is almost immediate. Your adjustment to the real world takes much longer. No time seems to have passed for your friends or family, and the date is one day later than your last day in the warehouse. Your body bears the scars, both mental and physical from the HR "exercises," but you are so glad to be out that you move on and try not to look back.

The End

"Charlie here is from a movie that was made years ago. This office belongs to our Chief Financial Officer, Ottis Toole. He handles all our bills and payments. Not sure why he had Charlie here in his office?" Grady says, putting the doll back on the desk. "Maybe someone else in finance was playing a prank on Ottis? They sometimes get carried away with their little games."

"Um, I think I need to sit down or take a break or something," you tell Grady, still a little scared from the screaming doll.

"So sorry that you got caught in their prank war!" Grady says, "but we really have a lot to do tonight! I could get you a pill for your nerves…it will make you feel better!"

"What's in the pill?" you ask, only considering it because of how upset you are. "Can I just lie down in the break room?" Maybe you don't need this job after all, and you can go home and never come back if you don't feel better soon?

"Well, I suppose so," Grady says, "but I'd prefer it if we got everything done first. The pill is just a homeopathic remedy, nothing dangerous or illegal!"

If you push Mr. Grady to let you lie down, thinking that you might instead just go home, turn to page 32.

If you choose to take the pill to settle your upset nerves, turn to page 63.

Pushing the trolley out of the way with all of your strength, you slam your shoulder against the door. But it doesn't break. You try again, and while it rattles in the frame, it holds firm. Wiping your brow, you look at the B-WARE unit.

"Of course!" you say out loud to yourself. Using the B-WARE as a battering ram, you get some speed and smash it into the door. The door splits in two but B-WARE gets lodged in the opening, blocking your way. It takes you a minute or two to pull it back out, meanwhile the screaming doesn't stop—it gets worse.

You crawl under the broken door into the dark room where the noise is coming from. Taking out your phone and putting it into flashlight mode, you look around. The noise is coming from the corner of the room, but it's empty. All you see is a large utility sink with water streaming out of the faucet. Maybe there is an animal trapped in the sink that is making the noise?

Approaching the sink cautiously, ready for a trapped rat or raccoon to snap, you shine the light into the basin. All you see is water swirling in a whirlpool down the drain.

OOOORROOWOOOOROOOOORRROOOR-RRR-yeeeeeeeeeeeeeee!!!!

The sound is coming from the water as it drains out of the sink! Turning both knobs to shut off the water, you relax as the scream stops when the last of the water empties.

Turn to page 22.

Sitting down on the floor with your back against the wall, you wonder how you'll explain the broken door to Mr. Grady. But you are relieved. The screaming was nothing bad.

Taking a few deep breaths and gathering yourself, you look around the room. Dirty laundry is heaped in the corners and piled in wheeled baskets. It looks like mostly sheets and towels. On the far wall, shelves are stocked with detergent and other cleaning supplies. Nothing too unusual. Then you look at the door. Since you broke only the bottom part of the door with the trolley, the top of the door is still closed and intact. The manual sliding lock is still in the locked position. The door was locked from the inside, and there is no other way out of this windowless laundry storage room. How is that possible?

"Okay, don't get freaked out," you say out loud to yourself. Then the pile of laundry in the corner starts to move!

Go on to the next page.

Backing towards the broken door, you are actually relieved when a huge rat with glowing red eyes comes scuttling out of the dirty sheets. It scurries up the wall and disappears into a black hole near the ceiling.

You move towards the pile the rat crawled from and pull off the top sheet. You jump back and give a little scream when you see four rat pups searching for their mother.

Turn to the next page.

"What are you doing?" a voice booms from the darkness behind you.

Another little scream escapes from you, and you swing around and aim your flashlight up. Your boss Mr. Grady squints back in the bright light.

"Sorry, I didn't mean to scare you," he says, "but why is the B-200 Powered Hand Truck smashed into the door?"

"I heard something screaming in here, but it was the sink's drain, and then I found rats...baby rats over there," you babble, pointing.

Grady laughs his sharp laugh, "Oh, the Haunted Sink! I should have warned you about that. It makes quite the racket! Certainly unnerving, I know. Well, no help for the door. We'll have to pull out a replacement and leave a note for the maintenance crew. As for the rats," he says, striding to the wall and flicking on the lights without looking, "we'll need to put out poison unfortunately. I've been meaning to deal with that but it keeps slipping my mind."

Go on to the next page.

"Which would you like to do, go get the poison or the door? The poison bucket is heavy but it is just down the hall from the locker room. The replacement door is in the Dahmer Annex on the far side of the property," he says, pointing to one of the windowless walls as though you could tell where he means. "These hollow-core doors are light enough for one person to carry, no problem, not like a dead body!" Grady laughs again, as if at a joke, but you don't join in.

If you choose to go get the poison bucket, turn to page 46.

If you decide to go and get the replacement door, turn to page 102.

You stand on a catwalk, high above the floor of a storage hanger. Large machines hulk below you in the purplish glow of the cheap mercury vapor lights. The countess stands behind you, with a long spear. She pokes it at you. You move away, but the catwalk ends.

"Now, climb toward the light!! If you make it, you get another test, but if you fall, then you'll be dead!"

You rush at the countess, batting aside the spear with a desperate strength. She just reaches out with one hand and you fall down, twitching.

"Now climb to the light!"

You climb towards the buzzing industrial light, but it is far away. Hand-over-hand, you inch forward. You hold on to a too-thin support, and you are only a few feet in when the metal dips and pulls away from the ceiling.

You fall to the floor…and wake up with Mr. Grady standing over you. He is sweaty and he looks scared.

"You're awake!" he says, grabbing your arm and helping you up. The room seems to be spinning. You were falling…

"What happened?" you both say at once.

Turn to the next page.

28

Mr. Grady takes a breath and says "You were just standing there, and *blam!* you mumbled something and fell to the floor!!"

"When did this happen?" you ask, thinking about the Brown Lady and the countess.

"Just now, not more than two minutes ago!" he replies.

"Maybe it was the pill you gave me?" you ask, shaking your head to clear it.

"But that was just a breath mint," he tells you. "Honestly!"

The End

"Here, take it," you say, handing over the whole key ring. The woman takes the master key off the ring and hands the rest back to you.

"Thanks," she says, pocketing the key. "This will be very useful. Johnson, please help this citizen out of the mansion. Use the most direct route. I'll wait for a while in the White Room, but I'll have to move on if you aren't back in 30 minutes."

"Got it," Agent Johnson replies. "Let's go, kid."

You follow Agent Johnson out of the door you originally came through. You pass by an empty indoor swimming pool and into a dusty and unused kitchen. The appliances look very old and non-functional.

"Why are you two here?" you ask Agent Johnson. "Who are you? What does 'like the FBI' mean?"

Johnson stops for a moment, turns, and looks you in the eye. "We hunt ghosts. Not like in the movies with marshmallow men. Real ghosts. Not the harmless ones that move ashtrays. Killers and torturers, those are the ghosts we hunt. Sometimes they hunt us back."

"I guess, I don't know, it sounds kind of crazy…" you say, before going silent. Maybe he's lying, maybe he's not, but something is definitely odd. Maybe there really are ghosts?

"You're part of it," Johnson says, stopping you.

"What do you mean?"

"You had Grady's master key. You're part of this."

Turn to the next page.

30

Johnson doesn't say any more and he moves out of the kitchen. You follow, just in time to see Johnson fall into a trapdoor that opens as he puts his weight on it.

Moving with elegant speed, Johnson kicks his legs out, drops the gun and grabs the edge of the trapdoor. He calmly pulls himself up to the edge and is bringing one of his legs up, when something pulls him down. He grunts in pain. Scrambling with his fingers, he grits his teeth and tries to grab onto something solid, but there is nothing nearby.

"No, NO! NOT YOU!" Johnson yells as he gets yanked into the trap. His eyes are scared as he drops backwards into the hole.

Not knowing what to do, you move carefully to the edge of the trapdoor. You can see the latch mechanism that held the door up, but beyond that is pure blackness. All you hear are scrabbly, skittery sounds, and then silence.

Moving backwards, you turn and run away. Retracing your steps, you make it back to the bedroom with the two chairs quickly. You decide you have to find the woman who was with Johnson. She has the key. All you want is to get out of here.

You follow the path of open doors until you hear shouts, yells and gunshots. Normally you would run in the other direction, but something inside of you tells you that going back would be worse.

Turn to page 54.

"Just lie down then," Mr. Grady says, pointing to a cot in a room near the employee locker room. "This is for when we need to work around the clock."

"Aren't we doing that? We're here at night and then the day shift comes in, right?" you ask as you sit on the cot.

"No, this is just a maintenance shift, you should see it when it gets really crazy! People bouncing off the walls! Working under death-lines. I'll come back in an hour, but then we need to really get back to work!"

"Okay," you say, lying down on top of the thin blanket. Mr. Grady closes the door to the small room, leaving you in darkness. You hear a *CLUNK*. It sounds like a bolt lock sliding into place. You hope that is not the case.

Stumbling forward in the darkness, you search for the light switch and the door at the same time. You find the switch first, turn on the lone bulb, and immediately try the door. The doorknob turns, but the door is still held fast. You are locked in!

Turn to page 59.

Leaving the B-WARE and running as fast as you can, you head towards Mr. Grady's office. By the time you get there, you are out of breath. Knocking on the door, you gulp in great big breaths of the humid summer air. There is no response, and no light shows beneath the door. Deciding that you can't wait, you give the doorknob a try and silently open the door to Mr. Grady's dark office.

Flicking on the light, you see Mr. Grady lying on the floor. He isn't moving.

"Mr. Grady?" you say, fear making your voice sound shrill in your own ears. "Are you okay? Mr. Grady?"

Gasping loudly, Mr. Grady sits up from the waist as though he were sitting in a car seat that is being brought up from a full recline. "What? Who?" he says, blinking and turning just his head towards you. His voice is dry and raspy.

"Mr. Grady," you say, "are you okay? Why are you on the floor? There's something screaming in one of the locked rooms."

"Huh?" he says. "What room? What kind of scream?"

"I don't know," you reply. "Down the hall, it sounds like someone, or something, is in pain!"

"Well, we don't want that!" he says, laughing. He uses the edge of his desk to pull himself up and shakes his leg and wiggles his foot. "Must have lost blood flow to my foot. I'll need a minute or two for the pins and needles to pass."

Turn to the next page.

34

"Take the master key," Mr. Grady says, handing you a large ring of keys. The key that he is holding is deep black, so black that it is shiny. "I'll be right behind you!"

You were hoping that Mr. Grady would go with you, but you have no choice but to run ahead by yourself. The sound has stopped, and you can't remember exactly which room it was coming from. They all look the same. You hear something coming from the hall behind you and you look over your shoulder to see a limping dark figure coming towards you. You feel a cold flush of fear. But then the figure passes under one of the dim lights and you see that it is just Mr. Grady.

You turn the lock of one of the doors and open it, glad that you are not completely alone. The room is dark and you fumble for the light switch. The screaming noise is coming from a metal desk in the middle of the room. It is a doll. A redheaded doll holding a knife in its left hand while screaming. The tiny mouth moves with the warbling of the howl. Backing away from the doll, you bump into Mr. Grady as he comes into the room.

"Oh, that's all it is!" Grady says as he moves past you and heads right to the doll. Picking it up, he turns it over and fumbles with the back for a second. The howling stops.

"What is that thing?" you ask, your voice shaking.

"It's just a doll!!" Grady says, walking towards you, holding out the creepy doll for your inspection. "Don't worry, Charlie won't hurt you! It isn't a real knife. Here, take a look."

Go on to the next page.

The doll's eyes are wide set with enormous pupils and its smiling mouth has red drops of blood trickling from the left side. Even though you can tell that the knife is plastic, you don't take the doll from Grady's outstretched hand.

Turn to page 19.

"You *have* been touched!"

You stand there shaking for minutes before pulling yourself together and going to find Mr. Grady. Enough is enough, after what happened tonight you know you are getting away from here. Mr. Grady doesn't seem surprised when you tell him what you saw and why you are leaving. He gives you 30 one-dollar coins in severance, counting them out one by one and giving his creepy laugh.

"Thirty pieces! Go then! You've been touched!"

You shiver.

Ever since that night, you have been touched. Why did you taunt the Brown Lady by grabbing at her? You aren't sure, but being "touched" is not all bad. Seeing ghosts all over the place is exhausting and often disturbing, as their deaths are usually violent or very, very sad. Ghosts are all very self-centered, they always want to talk about themselves, and they never ask how you are doing. However, you have learned to be more sympathetic to their plights. Your job as the foremost ghost whisperer (and exorcist if the need arises, which is thankfully rare!) relies on your special ability to see and communicate with the dead. When you do your job well the restless spirit finds a sense of peace and the humans who have to deal with it get relief. When the job goes poorly, things get hectic. Some of the images you have seen almost break you.

The End

"You promise that you'll help me find my mama's ring?" Mary says, inching slowly out of her hiding spot. She looks up at you and suddenly seems much older. "She's not really just my mama, you know. She's the mother of us all."

"'All' who?" you ask. "Are there other children in the warehouse?"

"Some," Mary answers. "As well as those who are no longer children. We are all ages, I guess, or any age."

"Okay," you agree, not knowing what she means. "But I have to get to work, so the sooner we find this ring, the better. Where did you last see it?"

"It is in a box, and the box is supposed to be in this room. It is a special box, made of sandalwood and cedar."

"Let's get searching," you say, wondering why you agreed to this. She seemed so persuasive!

You search the whole workshop, but come up empty-handed. Really *you* searched, Mary just watched and pointed out things to move. The only place you don't look is a drawer below the bench, locked with a simple combination lock.

"No dice, kiddo," you say. "We need to get out of here and find someone to come get you!"

"Please, just try the locked drawer!" she pleads. "It has to be in there!"

"It's locked for a reason," you counter.

Go on to the next page.

"Please!" implores Mary. She starts to cry. "I'll never be able to rest! Ever. None of us will. Just try it one time? I may know the code. I just want to see the ring for a second! You can put it right back! Please?"

"Okay," you say. "I'll give it one try! But no more messing around after that. You need to get to bed."

"I long for rest. Use 9696 in the lock. It is the same from up or down. Mama likes that."

You put the combination in and the lock springs open. Inside the drawer is a wooden box in the middle of a wicker basket. A peaceful smell pours into you. Gently, you pick up the box and open the lid. Inside, on a bed of purple velvet, is a simple ring made of jade. Even in the dim light, it glints with a green that draws the eye into its never ending circle.

"Oh!" Mary whispers. "Mama's ring! It's so pretty!"

You pick the green ring up to examine it closer, and before you can react, Mary puts her thumb through the ring. A flash of green light from the ring makes you blink, and when you open your eyes, Mary is glowing with the same green light. She smiles.

"Thank you! Now I can rest," she says and then slowly she fades away. The ring drops back into the box, and she is almost invisible, just a hint of an outline left, when the door slams open and Mr. Grady rushes in.

"What have you done!" Mr. Grady bellows. "Mary, what have you done!"

Turn to the next page.

You can barely see it, but Mary smiles wider, sticks out her tongue at Mr. Grady and fully disappears.

"You!" Mr. Grady yells, pointing at you. "You are in very big trouble! Mary is irreplaceable!"

He is so angry, you have never seen him like this and it is scary. He looks like he could murder you right now. His hands clench and unclench. He steps towards you, growling a little.

And then he begins to fade away, just as Mary did.

Mr. Grady stops and looks at his fading hand. The look on his face changes from anger to terror.

"No!!!" he moans. You hear the faint laughter of a young girl as Mr. Grady dissolves.

Then the shop slowly dissolves around you. In just a couple of minutes you are in a normal, well-lit parking lot by a small, very ordinary warehouse building. The whole complex is about a tenth the size of the warehouse that you entered earlier tonight. Completely by itself, your car is the only one in the parking lot. You get in and drive home.

The next day a package arrives. Inside it is a small white box, and inside the box, on a cushion of white satin, is a crystal ring. The ring is perfectly smooth, and you feel protected when you wear it. When you took it to a jeweler, she offered you $10,000 for the ring, even though she did not know what it was made of. You politely declined.

The End

You decide to become the leader of your team without knowing what it involves. Gripping the paintball gun tightly, you pop your head around the corner to get a quick peek at the team you've elected to lead. It's risky as no one is allowed any eye protection. They even made Evan take his glasses off. Without them he is almost blind. It is a real liability for your team. Normally Evan is one of your better teammates, but today you just hope he doesn't accidentally shoot one of his own team.

The view was clear, so you motion the remaining members of your squad to move forward. DeSean and Zihyang both got hit in an ambush earlier and they are watching from the observation booth. You have a one person disadvantage right now, plus Evan being a liability really makes you two down. The win is important. Everyone needs a good meal. It has been a couple of days since your team had a win. Even with a win, it still won't be enough food. All of you are so thin it hurts to look at each other.

Getting the win was great for your team. Even the beans and rice tasted amazing without any sauce or veggies, let alone meat. *How long have I been here, now?* you wonder. Definitely months. Maybe six months? You think of home all the time. *Do they think I'm dead? Did they have a funeral? What did they put in the coffin? I would kill, literally kill, for a pizza.*

Each day is some new pointless exercise. You battle other teams, whom you only see when competing. No one knows what is going on. You are all trapped in this underground complex.

Go on to the next page.

There are no clocks, just loud buzzers that seemingly go off randomly. Sometimes dinner and lunch are about an hour apart, other times it seems like ten or more hours pass between the two, but it is hard to know as there are no clocks.

Turn to the next page.

Just this week, you have been in a Scorpion and Worms eating challenge (you got a painful sting on your tongue) and played Ninja Knights Piñata. They gave you broomsticks, put "blaster helmets" on you, and left all of you in a bare room with piñatas hanging from the ceiling. You just wandered around swinging your broomstick blindly, sometimes you hit a piñata, or another person. Someone cracked you so hard in the ribs that you fell down. Your team lost because you did not get as much candy as the other teams. Supposedly if you do well at these "exercises," they'll let you out. But no one has gotten out so far. Each time a team comes close, HR changes the rules to deny a "transfer."

None of the games are overtly deadly, but all are dangerous, exhausting, disgusting or demeaning. You don't see Hepburn or Padurii. Mr. Franz Akfak, the gatekeeper, keeps the gate permanently closed. Whenever you ask for a meeting, he schedules it and then they cancel at the last minute. You've stopped trying.

How long will this continue? How long can you continue? You fall asleep hoping there was some way to get out of this prison. That night you dream that you are having a meeting with a nice woman in a normal office. People walk by and go about their business in a friendly way. It is nothing like your current reality.

Go on to the next page.

"Can you help me?" you ask her. The name on her desk says Tanya Garcia. She smiles and nods.

"Gnikool peek tsuj!" she says. It makes no sense to you.

"I can't understand you," you say. "I'm sorry!" She frowns.

"Ti rof kool ot evah uoy," she says, nodding vigorously, but it is gibberish to you. You shake your head.

"81 egap ot nrut 9696 :mroF a elif ot si tuo yaw ylno eht," she says. This time she says each word very slowly, but you still can't understand her.

You wake up frustrated. That day your team loses, and hunger dominates all your thoughts. Days stretch on. How long will this last?

The End? *Or is it?!*

"Take the master key," Mr. Grady says with a strange intensity, handing you a silver key with a gold finish on its head. A red letter O is stamped on it. "It will open any door in the complex. Do not lose it or allow it to fall into the wrong hands! I want you to put a scoop of poison in each of the rooms in this building. Except for the Forbidden Room. Don't go in there. It is clearly marked, and there are things that could be...unhealthy for you if you open that door."

"Okay-kay-kay," you stammer. "What's in there? And why does the key have an 'O' on it?"

"The 'O' is for 'Original,' and there are delicate experiments going on in the Forbidden Room, what else?" Mr. Grady laughs. "Don't go in there."

He hands you the key, and it is oddly heavy for its size. *Poison! This job stinks!* you think to yourself, but out loud you say, "Don't worry, Mr. Grady, I'll get the poison and I won't go into the Forbidden Room."

"Great, I'll go get the door and come right back."

You take the key and find the supply room. A bench of sorts holds scales, beakers, test tubes and bags filled with powders. There's a chemical odor in the air.

"*This* should be called the Forbidden Room," you mutter to B-WARE. In the corner is a five-gallon bucket with a skull and crossbones and the words RAT POISON written on the lid in red marker.

Go on to the next page.

Scooting down the hallway with the B-WARE cart and a bucket of poison is more fun than you thought it would be. You make good progress as you move through the warehouse. Taking the scoop, you put some of the blue pellets in the corner of each of the rooms, trying to put it in a place where rats would be likely to scurry and where people would maybe not notice it.

Turn to the next page.

Most of the rooms are pretty ordinary. You glance over ordinary boxes labeled things like "Castle Financials 1592-1648" or "Artifacts from Mary Celeste: Captain's Log incl." They are stacked in neat rows. Some rooms don't have boxes at all. One has racks and racks of gowns and dresses. They look pretty nice, but you suppose they would need to be if they are being sent out for movie productions. A number of them are torn or stained.

The strangest room has all sorts of masks. Some are just party masks of animals like wolves, birds, or cats, or simple face coverings with holding-sticks and feathers. But there are hundreds of scary masks on foam heads. Zombies, ghouls, ghosts, aliens and tentacled monsters stare at you with empty eyes. Feeling a little creeped out, you dump a scoop of poison in the corner and get out of there as quickly as you can.

Go on to the next page.

Your bucket is halfway gone and you have been to most of the rooms in the building, as far as you can tell. (You were careful to skip the Forbidden Room, which was clearly marked. You pushed back the desire to take just a quick look inside.) You pause in front of a door that is labeled "Animal Control: AUTHORIZED PERSONNEL ONLY!!" Mr. Grady did tell you "every room" but you still consider skipping it. Without conscious thought you find yourself opening the door anyway. You immediately regret it.

Turn to the next page.

A huge dog, like a wolfhound but even bigger, is gorging on a large piece of meat on the floor. It looks up and stares at you with glowing eyes. Its muzzle is covered in blood, and you freeze. You see what it is eating. It looks like one of those haunches they feed lions in zoos, but why is the dog eating it in the middle of the room? Gobbets of bloody meat are scattered all over the floor.

Go on to the next page.

Cages filled with cats, birds, and screaming monkeys line the wall. You see a cage with the free dog's twin, and next to that, a cage with its door bent open. You have to get out of here! The dog rears and leaps toward you, growling, and you try to escape and slam the door behind you, but the dog is too fast and powerful. You push the B-WARE cart at the dog, but the animal jumps over the cart and escapes the room. The dog knocks the poison bucket over and spills the blue pellets all over the floor of the hallway. You run back the way you came.

Right in front of you is the red door of the Forbidden Room. You still have the master key in your hand. Looking further down the hallway, you see a ladder leading up into the ceiling. If you could make it there, then the dog wouldn't be able to climb after you. You hope. It is only about 15 yards away, but the dog is coming at you quickly, and low growls are coming from its bloody maw.

If you decide to go into the Forbidden Room, even though Mr. Grady specifically warned you against it, turn to page 74.

If you try to make a run for the ladder leading up and away from the bloody dog and the unknown risks in the Forbidden Room, turn to page 85.

52

Lighting the fire takes most of the matches in the pack, but you finally get the twigs burning in a sustained flame. Adding fuel slowly, you build the tiny fire into a good-size blaze. You lean back against the moss covered boulders and warm yourself by the bonfire until you start to feel better. The light and the heat make your situation seem a little less crazy. All of those "Survive-in-the-Wilderness" shows stress staying warm as the number one priority.

Then you see something moving in the darkness beyond the fire's light.

Turn to page 113.

You are afraid, but you don't move. You cannot run any longer, as you are too tired to continue. The flying host gallops down at you. The rider launches its spear, but at that moment, the first ray of dawn strikes from the far horizon. With no noise or any other indication that the murderous host was just there, they disappear. You are alone on top of your boulder, and the sunrise is the most beautiful of your whole life.

From that moment on, you gain a confidence in yourself that allows you to achieve great things. There is no sign of Malik, Sarah or the cabin, but you know you did not dream what happened.

The End

You come to a grand glass double-doorway that leads into a ballroom. Peering into the ballroom, you see the woman who took the master key, Agent Johnson's partner, firing her gun at a swirling mass of darkness that has the contorted face of an angry man. Broken glass covers most of the white marble floor. Smoke billows up from the far end of the room, and you see a few bright flames through the chaos. A high keening sound comes out of the ghost's mouth, and you put your hands over your ears to block it.

The woman calmly tucks the gun into her holster and draws out a darkly gleaming steel tomahawk. In one smooth motion, she pulls her arm back and releases the tomahawk straight at the face of the keening ghost. It hits the ghost square in the face and then you lose sight of it. The keening sound stops, but the ghost pulls in toward the woman for a moment before dissipating into nothingness.

Turn to the next page.

56

The woman loses all the color in her face and she crumples to the ground. Smoke from the fires makes you cough as you creep towards her. She is shaking and holding the master key tightly in her right hand.

"Where's Johnson?" she asks, weakly.

"He's...gone," you answer. "We have to get you out of here before the smoke gets us. Does that really lead to the outdoors?"

"Yes, but it's too late for me. The spirit of the chief got me. This is his roost. I got him first though," she coughs and is silent for a moment. "He didn't like that I stole his tomahawk, Night Breaker."

"We have to get out of here. I'm not leaving you to die," you say, holding your shirt over your mouth and nose. You learned that line from a movie. "Give me the key and I'll try and drag you with me."

"Look kid, I'm dead, it's over for me, but you have to find that tomahawk! It's the only thing powerful enough to destroy the master key! Without the key, they'll be stuck. No more playtime for Grady and his spook pals. You have to do it!"

If you decide to get away from the fire, save the agent, and escape the haunted mansion, turn to page 61.

If you choose to look for Night Breaker and use it to destroy the master key, turn to page 94.

"Or?" you ask when Mr. Grady pauses for what you consider to be too long.

"Or, you can talk to my boss, the head of this warehouse, and have any questions you have answered to the best of our ability."

"What's the catch?"

"Knowledge is power, that is true, but sometimes we should not want to know everything. The truth can be...disturbing. There are things that should remain unknown."

"Like what?"

"This is but a small example, consider it merely as indicative, but do you want to know everything that you have eaten by accident? While true, you may not find it appetizing," Mr. Grady says, before changing his tone to a more business-like one. "The hour is late and we have gotten almost none of the scheduled work done for the night. What do you wish to do? Are you the monkey who has to know, or are you the sheep, willing to graze in obliviousness?"

If your curiosity and demand for knowledge outweighs your desire for home, turn to page 9.

If you decide to get out of the warehouse and never come back, turn to page 93.

You search the small room, but there is no way out.

Having nothing better to do, you lie down on the cot. Soon you are asleep. Rats are gnawing at you in your dreams. Your hands are covered in bites from the vermin…

You wake to a man and woman you don't know standing over you, staring down. He is youngish, in his thirties, and almost skeletally thin. She is old, with a grumpy face and squinting eyes. Both have stern looks. They are wearing professional business attire, blue suits, but both also have dark red roses pinned to their lapels. The woman holds a manila folder in her hands. You see your name on the label.

"Good, you're awake," says the man. "My name is James Hepburn, and this is my associate, Muma Padurii. We're from Human Resources. The home office sent us." He sounds English.

"Good morning," the woman says. She speaks perfect English, but still sounds Eastern European, maybe Romanian?

"Huh?" you mumble, sitting up. Your hands are bite free, and that makes you glad. "What are you talking about?"

"Well, Mr. Grady advised us that you were thinking about leaving our firm and we came to talk to you about it. In fact, we believe that after you speak with us, you'll reconsider your decision," Ms. Padurii says.

"It's just a summer job. I'm just a kid. Mr. Grady locked me in here! That's illegal! I quit and I want a lawyer!"

Turn to the next page.

"I'm sorry you feel that way," Mr. Hepburn says, "but that is not really possible. You signed an employment contract. Why don't you calm down?"

"Don't tell me to calm down," you say, your voice rising. "This is ridiculous! I'm out of here!"

"Calm down!" the old woman snaps at you and you fall silent. "You have no choice. Contract was signed. If you continue, I will make a note in your file. You do not want a second note in your file." She holds her pen threateningly above the folder with your name.

"Go ahead, fire me!"

"Enough of this," Mr. Hepburn says, breaking in. "Let's move on. Anyway, due to your attitude, we're going to do some team-building exercises. This will help you bond with your co-workers, as well as provide tools for problem-solving."

"Is this a joke? Ha ha, not funny. I don't have any 'co-workers' except for Mr. Grady."

"No joke," says Ms. Padurii. "Soon you will meet your co-workers. You do have a choice to make, though."

"Yes, most assuredly!" says Mr. Hepburn, breaking into a disturbing smile. "Life is full of choices! So, are you management or labor?"

"What?"

"Excuse Mr. Hepburn," Ms. Padurii says, shooting him a nasty look. "He married into royalty, he has a hard time sympathizing with the common folk. I treat all the same. Except for children, I love children!"

Turn to page 67.

"Come on, we're getting out of here," you say, grabbing the woman's collar and right arm. You pull her across the ballroom floor, staying low to avoid the smoke. She is surprisingly light and she slides easily across the slick floor of the ballroom.

"No, no, no!" she moans. "Get the tomahawk, destroy the master key!"

"Sorry, lady, I don't want to die, and I don't want you to die. I just want to get out of this crazy place!" you say as you reach the glass doors leading outside. The master key opens the lock with a smooth click and you push the doors open. Smoke billows out as you pull the woman behind you. You pick her up and put her on your shoulder. Stumbling, you half fall down the broad steps to the garden before falling down on a grassy spot.

"We made it!" you say, coughing from the smoke inhalation, but you are so glad to be out of the haunted building! The woman does not respond. You check on her.

She is not breathing and her open eyes are glassy and unfocused. You feel for a pulse. Nothing. You start CPR, hoping that you are doing it correctly. After a few breaths, an EMT taps you on the shoulder and takes over. You did not notice the sirens and lights until now. Another EMT gives you an oxygen mask after asking you the standard questions: Are you injured? Where? Can you move? You watch the firemen battle the flames. They pour foam and water all over the building and they have it mostly under control by the time they load you into the ambulance.

Turn to the next page.

The unnamed woman you met with Agent Johnson doesn't survive, even with CPR from you and the EMT. The official cause was listed as "cardiac arrest caused by hypothermia." She had no identification on her and no one came to claim the body. They called her "Jane Doe" and put her in a municipal cemetery lot.

The police hold you as a juvenile suspect for the arson, but you know they think you either killed the woman or somehow caused her death. "Who was the woman you were with? Did you have an altercation? Did you set the mansion on fire? How did you set the fire? Do you know how much damage you caused? Did you kill 'Jane Doe'? How did you kill her? Why did you run away? How did you get to California from your home?"

Your parents fly out to get you, and they have questions of their own, but theirs are asked out of love and concern. Everything you tell them is the truth as far as you know it. No one is satisfied with your answers, including you.

Eventually the police let you go. Your parents confront the owners of the warehouse, but there is no record that Mr. Grady worked there. However, a final paycheck reaches you just a few weeks after you return home—and it's more money than you would have made over many years in Mr. Grady's employ. Your parents suspect it's a settlement to hush up any bad publicity, but you all decide to keep it anyway. It doesn't keep your bad memories of your days at the warehouse at bay, but it does help you to keep your gas tank full.

The End

You take the small white pill from Mr. Grady and choke it down without any water.

Almost immediately, you feel a soothing warmth spread from the middle of your being to the tips of your tingling fingers.

"Better?" Grady asks with a lopsided smile. "Now we can get back to work! Lots to do before morning! We have all sorts of...productions going on in the next few nights!"

"Sure," you respond, slurring a little. "Let's go!"

The next few hours pass in a pleasant haze. All of your worries from before have dissolved into the warmth of the pill. *What was it?* you wonder, but not in a way that really matters. You move boxes, crates, pallets and racks from one part of the warehouse to another. You are productive and happy. You zip along with your friend the B-WARE electric hand cart, or you have the strength to lift many boxes by yourself! Time seems to slow and speed up at the same time. Part of you feels that you have only just begun, while another feels like you have been doing this task for days, months, years and centuries. You hum a happy little song to yourself, "What a great guy Mr. Grady is!"

Then everything starts to darken. At first you think it is just the lights, but they stay at the same brightness. Things seem thicker, darker, scarier. Your heart beats faster.

Turn to the next page

You look up and around you. You are in a large stage area somewhere deep below the main complex. The ceiling rises high above you, and boxes are piled all around, but directly in front of you is a trailer-sized wheeled platform with a grand staircase set in its middle.

The broad marble steps lead down to a black and white checkered floor. The only lights in the large room are from weak bulbs widely set apart high above. Everything is dim. Except for the woman in the brown dress floating down the staircase.

"Who are you?" you squeak, dropping the box you had in your hands and backing away from the advancing glowing woman in the brown dress. She does not say anything. Her face is mostly covered by a veil, but her eyes appear as empty holes of blackness. You notice that the brown dress sparkles too-brightly in the dim light. She reaches the bottom of the stairs and floats over the checkered floor towards you.

Turn to the next page.

Stumbling backwards, you bump into the back wall. You look over at the door, but the woman in the brown dress has left the platform and has floated most of the distance across the floor to where you are. You are shaking.

Reaching around desperately, you find a broom that is leaning against the wall. Grabbing it in your hands you hold it in front of you like a sword.

"Stop!" you yell, and the figure pauses for a moment before moving towards you again.

What do you do?

If you choose to attack the floating brown ghost with the broom, turn to page 78.

If you decide not to anger the ghost by attacking, and instead try to talk to the ghost, turn to page 98.

You shudder. She is creepy. Her eyes glow with hunger and she licks her lips in a way that reminds you of a wolf. Who are these people? Maybe you can force your way out of the door? As if reading your mind, Mr. Hepburn pushes the door closed with his foot and stands in front of it.

"You'll be in team-building exercises all day and you will be judged on your performance," he says. "This is very important for your place in the firm. Do not fail. So, you must choose. Do you want to be the team leader or do you just want to be part of the team? If you are leader, you will get a better reward if you succeed. If you fail, your punishment will be more...severe. As I said before, management or labor?!"

You don't want to take part in the exercises, whatever they are. The whole thing is bizarre, illegal and scary. Maybe you should just be part of the team and try not to do anything stupid? But if you do that you won't be able to control what your team, whomever that is, does. What if the leader is incompetent and you fail as a result?

If you decide to become the "leader" for the HR team-building exercises, turn to page 42.

If you choose to be part of the team and not risk the more "severe" punishment, turn to page 116.

"Fire might be my favorite," the countess tells you. "The light, the heat, the smell of burning flesh, it all warms me to the depths of my soul. The only problem is no blood. Always sacrifices!"

"You're the one who killed all those children in your castle, centuries ago! You're a monster!" you yell.

"Of course I am," she says with a light laugh, tossing a burning brand from the brazier at her side directly towards your face.

Go on to the next page.

You are standing atop a pole on a small wooden platform in the middle of a castle's courtyard. Below you, at the base of the pole, a fire made of bundles of sticks burns with a sharp heat that hits you in waves. Oddly, the waves of smoke do not appear to coincide with those of heat. You duck the flaming missile.

"Oh good," the countess squeals, clasping her hands together like an excited five-year-old. "We have one who wants to play!"

Using a pair of tongs, she grabs another burning brand and carefully places it into a flared metal scoop on the end of a stick and launches it at you. This one misses low and falls into the fire below you. Normally you are not one for trash talk, but you figure that you have nothing to lose by taunting her. Maybe she'll get mad and keep missing?

"Air ball! Nice shot, Countess!" you yell. "Waiting for the fire to do your work for you?"

Turn to the next page.

70

The countess does not respond. Instead she calmly loads another missile into her launcher. Just as she is about to let go, a bony hand grabs her forearm. The burning brand pops forward a few feet and sputters in a small puddle in the courtyard. The thick wooden door behind her opens and you see the dark figure of Mr. Grady come out, look dismissively at the soldiers, and proceed towards the countess with long strides. He seems taller. He also seems angry.

"Enough, Countess," Mr. Grady says, taking the launcher from her unprotesting hand. "Go back to your demesne."

"But, Grady..."

"No 'buts,' Countess, and it's Mister Grady, Sir, to you! I outrank you by three degrees," Mr. Grady says, before letting her go and pointing at the two attendants. "You and you, douse that fire and get him down from there. Countess, remove yourself now! If you don't, I'll lock you back up."

"Fine," she huffs, and turns to go. Her soldiers bring out buckets and douse the fire. Mr. Grady helps you down from the pole with a ladder. Everything goes dark.

Turn to page 72.

You are back in Mr. Grady's dingy office in the warehouse. The chipped mug full of acrid instant coffee shakes against your lips as you slurp down the too-hot liquid.

"Are you okay?" Mr. Grady asks. His mug sits untouched on his desk. You think of a talk-show host interviewing his guest.

"Okay? No, I don't think I'm okay. What was that? What is going on here? Who are you? What the heck was 'the countess'? Please tell me this is a dream. Can I go home?"

"No, this is not…a dream, and yes, you can go home. As to the other questions, you have a choice to make about that. What happened tonight was not…planned. Or desired."

You stare at Mr. Grady for a while. His eyes are dark and he still seems much larger than before, but not any bigger physically, just more of a presence. "Thank you, I guess, you know, for saving me from her," you say after taking another large swig of horrid coffee. "From the countess, I mean."

Go on to the next page.

"You're welcome, but I would be a horrible supervisor if I let you be annihilated while on the clock!" Mr. Grady gives his usual creepy laugh. You shiver even though the sticky summer heat is making you sweat. He seems to realize that you don't appreciate the humor and stops his laughter short before continuing in a more sober tone. "You were supposed to be introduced to the...quirks...of this job gradually, not in such a dramatic and scary manner. So, you get a choice that few, if any, have ever had."

"What choice?"

"You can either go home, never to return. Your memories will gradually fade and you'll consider this to be a particularly vivid dream. Eventually even that will fade, but trust me, this is no dream."

Turn to page 57.

The ladder is too far, you could be mauled! Without hesitating, you rush to the door of the Forbidden Room and shove the master key into its lock. Turning the key and dashing through, you slam it closed. A whirring noise comes from the door. Breathing hard, you listen to the dog snarling and growling on the other side of the thick door. After only about a minute, the dog goes silent. *It probably went back to its meal,* you think, but you decide to wait it out before checking to see if it is gone. You look around and take in the Forbidden Room.

You are standing in a clean, windowless room. It's small and rectangular, well-lit by soft, indirect lighting. It's staged like a formal Victorian sitting room and seems completely out of place in this warehouse of endless storage spaces. Four portraits adorn the walls. Below each portrait is a small brass name plate. On the left side, the portraits are of two women. Both are young and pretty. The first woman is shown opening a sealed urn and the other is biting into an apple. The first is labeled "Pandora" and the second is "Eve."

Go on to the next page.

On the other wall are portraits of two different men. The first is a young man, his face turned upward. Beads of sweat cover his face and he looks strained. He is called "Icarus." The other portrait is of a late-middle-aged nobleman. He is wearing a velvet doublet and an ermine cape. He is large, with a dark-black beard that glints with blue highlights. His eyes are tight and suspicious. He is named "Bluebeard."

"One of these things is not like the other…" you mumble-sing to yourself. You turn around to open the door a crack to see if the dog is still there. It doesn't budge; it's locked. No problem, didn't Mr. Grady's master key get you in here? It will get you back out, right?

Turn to page 79.

"Fine," you say. "What do you want to do, Sarah?"

"I think Malik is right in this case. Good luck!"

You jog down the other path at a steady pace. You come to a clearing on top of a hill that gives you a good view. You see the lake and the outline of a mountain. The colored lights head away from you, toward the road that Malik took. The lights dive toward the ground and disappear. You hear three sharp blasts of the horn, then the howling and yipping of excited hounds. Trying not to think what that may mean, you take off towards the mountain.

Later, you hear the horn and the yipping and howling again. You shudder and keep going. The terrain becomes steeper, and the moonlight is more consistent, but the trees start to thin out. There is not a lot of cover. You hear the horn, and it seems like it is very near. Looking over your shoulder, you see the lights closing in on you. Exhausted beyond belief, you scramble to the top of a boulder, grab a fist-sized rock, and turn to face the hunt.

You see helmeted beings riding horses made of light, wielding spears and bows. The Stag-Horned figure in front blows the three sharp horn blasts, and the host descends out of the sky straight towards you. You can see the black steam coming from the nostrils of the light-horses and one of the ghost riders lifts its arm back to throw a spear. You respond by hurling your rock, but it falls well short of the nearest rider.

Turn to page 53.

Cocking back the broomstick, you swing it without warning, but you don't put your whole body into it as you know ghosts are supposed to be ethereal beings…sometimes. The broomstick passes through the body of the Brown Lady without any resistance.

"Crud," you say, then, trying to make the best of a bad situation: "Uhm, sorry about that!"

"You will PAY for that INDIGNITY!" the Brown Lady screeches at you. She floats towards you, hands outstretched. You wait in fear, not moving, but the Brown Lady seems to be slowing as she nears you. "Run while you can!" She wiggles her hands threateningly.

There is a clear path to the door leading away, and the Brown Lady hovers as if politely waiting her turn to go through. Why? Dropping the broomstick, you decide to stay still and see what happens.

"You can't touch me? Can you?" you say. "You don't have power over the real world, all you can do is scare people. Why do you do it?"

"Do not TEMPT me mortal! I came back from DEATH to avenge the wrongs done to me!" she hisses, staring at you with her empty holes of eyes. You shiver despite trying to appear brave.

Reaching forward quickly with your hand, you watch as the Brown Lady snatches her arm away from you. She backs away.

"Your connection to the real world is thinly bound," she spits at you as she floats away, before turning and putting her finger to your forehead. You feel nothing. She removes it and recedes.

Turn to page 36.

You put the silver master key into the lock of the Forbidden Room door. It turns the lock, but the door won't open. Desperate, you try every key on the chain, but none of them control the bolt that has been thrown.

"Hey! Mr. Grady!" you shout, banging your fist on the door. "Come let me out!"

You bang on the door and shout for at least five minutes, but there is no response, not even from the dog. Looking around the small room, you realize there is a second door out. You know it is just your imagination, but the people in the portraits seem to be waiting for you to step through it and into the unknown. You follow their gaze and try the far door. It's also locked, but it opens easily when you use the master key.

"Hopefully I'll be like Bluebeard's wife and someone will charge in to rescue me!" you whisper to yourself as you open the door onto a long hallway. The floor is wooden, and the corridor is lit by scalloped wall sconces holding flickering incandescent bulbs. The light is orangeish and the paper-covered walls look yellow, but it is hard to be sure in the light. You start opening up doors and going into rooms. Most are completely empty, but a few have antique furniture in them. Everything is very fancy and completely out of place from what you've seen so far in the warehouse. Rooms lead off from one another, doors open to brick walls, and a set of stairs lead to a deadly fall down a dark chute.

Turn to the next page.

80

You try and trace your steps back to where you started, but you can't seem to do it. Hours pass. Hunger and fear pick at you as you go from room to room. The master key works on all of the doors you come to, but you still can't get out. You start to run from room to room.

Rushing into yet another room, you are shocked to see two people on either side of an interior doorway: a blond man in a suit and a red-haired woman wearing a suit and a tight bun in her hair. Your relief to see other humans turns to terror when you take in their icy glares and the guns they hold. They both raise their weapons. Without conscious thought, you raise your hands.

"Please, don't shoot!" you croak.

The man lowers his gun. The woman holds her stance for a moment before lowering her gun and holding a finger to her lips. She gestures at you with her gun to move back, so you do.

You back through the empty room behind you and into a small bedroom with two chairs and a canopied and quilted queen bed that takes up most of the space. The woman comes into the room first, followed by the man, who closes both doors. She motions and you sit in one of the plush chairs.

"Who are you?" the woman asks quietly but with urgency. She doesn't smile. Neither of them point their guns at you, but neither of them put their guns away.

Turn to page 82.

"I'm just a kid! I'm trying to get out of here! Who are you two?"

"Where'd you get that key?" she asks. "What do you know about it?"

"Huh? Mr. Grady gave it to me. He said not to go into the Forbidden Room, but I had no choice, I was chased by a dog! That's all I know!"

"You know Grady!" the woman says excitedly, sending a look at her partner. He shrugs. "This is Grady's master key?"

"Yeah, he's my boss, but I just want to go home. Who are you?"

"We're like the FBI," she says, brushing you off.

"Can you help me then?" you ask, wishing they would put the guns away.

"Maybe, what do you think, Agent Johnson?"

"Key," he says, with a light accent that you can't place.

"Correct," the woman says to Agent Johnson before turning back to you. "Listen kid, we need that key."

"I just want to go home!"

"I have a deal for you. If you give me that key, I'll have Agent Johnson here escort you out of this maze. Without him, you'll wander for days. Part of this place is Winchester's mansion, you know, Winchester Repeating Arms, the gun manufacturer? The other half is the Chicago World's Fair Murder House. You don't want to be in either place. Both are made to confuse."

Go on to the next page.

"What if I don't give you the key? How do I know you aren't going to do something…horrible with it?"

"Look, kid," the woman answers, raising her gun slightly, "if we wanted to be jerks, we'd just take the key and leave you here, but we're on a mission. I need Johnson for what we are about to do. Without him, I will probably die a nasty death, but if you give me the key I can bypass that nastiness and I can spare Johnson while he gets you out of here. Trust me, you'll need his help."

If you think that keeping the master key instead of handing it over to armed strangers is your best choice, turn to page 16.

If you decide to give the unknown woman and Agent Johnson the master key in exchange for escort out, turn to page 29.

Without pausing to think, you sprint for the ladder, hoping that you will make it before the dog catches you. You start climbing, but in your haste, you slip as you reach for the rungs. Banging your head against the metal of the ladder, you turn to see that the dog has nearly reached you. With a burst of fear-inspired energy, you grab the rungs and pull yourself up the ladder. Once at the top, you pause in the darkness and look down.

The dog is going nuts. It is jumping and trying to climb the ladder itself. It makes it awfully close to your peering face. You can smell the blood and wet fur of the barking animal. You see the keys below the dog; you must have dropped them when you climbed up.

Backing away from the opening, you take a look around. You are in a cramped access area above the ceiling. The only light comes from cracks in the ceiling from the rooms below you.

Maybe the dog will go away? you think to yourself hopefully, but the crazed animal keeps leaping and barking. Surely Mr. Grady will hear and come looking? You wait for a while, but no one comes. You decide you must find another way out, and you turn on your phone to use as a flashlight. You have to hold it in your teeth and crawl through the cramped access area. You try to head in the direction you know the main office is in, but the metal supports you are climbing over don't lead that way.

Turn to the next page.

Following the only path, you calm down a little bit as the sounds of the crazy dog become fainter as you move away from it. You are thinking about trying to pry open part of the ceiling just to see where you are when you see the head of a second ladder poking up at the far end of the corridor you are in.

Crawling as fast as you can, you get to the ladder and scramble down it into a storage room. The room is tiny, with coiled ropes stacked all over the place. Most of the ropes are thick and made of natural fibers, but others look like professional rock-climbing equipment. There are two doors, one an emergency exit labeled with an "ALARM WILL SOUND" warning, and an ordinary-looking metal door. You try the metal door leading in, but it is locked with a combination lock. You have no choice except to use the emergency exit and sound the alarm. You wait for a moment before taking a deep breath and pushing the bar.

Go on to the next page.

The door opens much more easily than you expect and you fall forward and realize that you really are falling!

You hit the dirt below you with a hard THUMP! and your phone flies out of your hand. Its light shows the emergency door, about five feet above where you landed, closing with a click.

"This is STUPID!" you shout as you slowly get up, wiping dirt from your mouth and picking up your phone. "Who makes an emergency exit that opens up five feet above the ground?"

You realize that it is really cold, and your stomach tightens. Where are you? It feels like it is below freezing. It was hot and humid when you came to work, and now a cold dry wind is making you shiver.

Turn to the next page.

88

You are in a gully, with the building taking up one full side of it. The emergency door is the only break in a wall of brick blocking off the whole area. Dark trees hug both sides of the gully, blocking any way towards the rest of the building.

Shivering, you turn around. All you can see from the light of your phone are the twisted dark shapes of trees and black chunks of rock. The wind makes the trees in the distance sway with an eerie rhythm.

Jumping up to pound on the door warms you a little, but you realize that no one is going to come get you from the warehouse. You have to get out of here—wherever "here" is—on your own.

The gully pushes you away from the warehouse and you are glad to get away from it, but the forest is dark and foreboding. You have never felt more alone in your life.

The rocks are covered in a soft green moss, but are sharp nonetheless. There are so many fallen trees and clumps of rock that you spend most of your time climbing or crawling. Soon you are completely disoriented, with no idea which direction the warehouse is. Your phone shows only 8% of a charge and the flashlight app drains it quickly. The only good thing is that the wind has died down. It is still really cold. Your breath is visible, and when you breathe in, you feel the cold deep in your lungs. Even without the wind, the black trees in the distance still sway.

Turn to page 90.

90

The only good thing is that you have a pack of matches in your pocket from dinner. Your mom likes candles at dinnertime, and it is your job to light the candles. "Thanks, Mom," you whisper. What if you never see her again?

Your phone goes to 7% and you turn the flashlight off. Waiting a few moments for your eyes to adjust to the night, you open them and see nothing but darkness. Nothing. You can't see anything without the flashlight. It is cold and your light is running out. Maybe you should start a fire and wait for the morning? That seems like a reasonable idea: warmth and light are good things to have, but part of you screams to keep moving. You are familiar with the area of your town the warehouse is in, and you don't recognize any of this.

The further you can get away from the warehouse, the better. Crazy dogs, crazy Mr. Grady, crazy forest; you just want to get home. What should you do?

If you decide to stop, make a fire, set up shelter and wait for the morning, turn to page 52.

If you choose to keep moving through the forest to get as far from the haunted warehouse as possible, turn to page 108.

You're not sure what to do. Mr. Grady is waiting for you to come back with the door, and you still have the rest of the boxes to move tonight. You really don't have time to deal with a hiding kid in the middle of this crazy warehouse complex. Where did she come from and how did she get in here? The door to the shop was locked when you got here.

What should you do? Really, you know the right and proper thing would be to take her back to the main building and call the police. You would use your cell, but the whole area is a big dead zone and you have to use the landline in Grady's office.

But she seemed to get scared when you mentioned Grady. Maybe you should just help her find her ring, and if you don't find it in a few minutes you can take her to the office then?

If you choose to help Mary look for the ring, turn to page 38.

If you tell Mary that you won't tell on her, but that you need to call someone to let them know she is here, turn to page 120.

"Mr. Grady, I just want to go home."

"I understand, you must be as tired as a corpse!" he laughs. You don't.

Not bothering to get the few things you have in the warehouse, you sprint to the parking lot. You "accidentally" peel out as you drive away from the warehouse into the warm darkness of the night. How will you ever forget what happened tonight? It doesn't seem possible to forget the bathtub of blood.

Eventually the memory does fade. You transition from believing that you dreamed the whole experience in the warehouse to not remembering it at all. Years pass, life goes on. Castles and charcoal barbecues make you sweat nervously, and sometimes you wake up feeling like you are burning and choking on smoke. Only once did you wake up in the attic, amidst the wasteland of your old financial records scattered around you. How could a pay stub for $1500.00 from "Spectrum Specialty Warehouse, LLC" with the note: "Hazard Pay Bonus: Countesses" mean anything if you never worked for a company like that? It doesn't make any sense.

The End

You shuffle on your hands and knees through broken glass on the ballroom floor while smoke fills the vast room. One of the interior walls is fully engulfed in flames. You can still see the bright sunlight out of the windows and you figure you have a little time before the smoke becomes deadly.

The smoke clears for a moment and you see the tomahawk! Shuffling as fast as you can, you reach for it. It is covered in a foul-smelling green goo, but you pick it up anyway. Holding down the master key with one hand, you bring the blade of the black steel tomahawk down with as much force as possible.

The key breaks in two, and a flash of intense cold knocks you back. Picking yourself up, you look around. Everything, including you, is covered with a coating of ice. The fire is out and the smoke is gone. You look out the windows, but the sunlight is gone. A nothingness gapes from the glass. Not gray, not black, not white, just nothing.

Still holding the tomahawk, you shake as much ice off yourself as you can and move towards the woman. She is still breathing. Her ice covered eyes open. She smiles.

"It worked! I wasn't sure if it would!" she says, sounding stronger than before. She struggles to sit up. You help her.

"Now what?" you ask her. "How do we get out of here?"

"I'm not sure that we do," she says. "I'm Smith. Agent Smith, I mean, Amanda. That's my first name."

Go on to the next page.

"I think you're in shock, Amanda," you tell her. "Can you stand up?"

"Maybe," she responds, wiping ice off her, and struggling to stand.

Turn to the next page.

"We need to get out of here," you say. "I can't stand seeing that nothingness out the windows."

"Try walking backwards," Amanda says, after you have searched through all the rooms that you can get to in the mansion. She knows most of it pretty well, but it is confusing with the dead ends, doors to nowhere and stairs that end in brick walls. Her earlier suggestion was to smash every mirror you came to with the tomahawk, Night Breaker. All you have to show for that is a bunch of broken glass with silver backing. You are hungry, tired and thirsty. "Ghosts are very straight-forward beings. They aren't original thinkers. Here, eat this energy bar," she says, handing you a wrapped bar.

"Thanks," you say, walking backwards through the rooms you have been through multiple times. This time you see a full-length mirror that was not there before. You immediately swing Night Breaker at it and instead of shattering, the mirror pops like a bubble. On the other side is the hall that you originally entered the mansion from. It feels like that was years ago.

"Follow me. I think I know where I am," you tell Amanda, stepping through the hole where the mirror was.

The door in the room with the cot is still dead-bolted, but it smashes open with one swing from Night Breaker. Everything in the warehouse is silent and a thick layer of dust covers everything. You hold the tomahawk up in case you run into Mr. Grady, a ghost, or something even more terrible.

Go on to the next page.

Moving silently down the dusty hallways, you rush to the nearest exit.

Outside, it is night, and it is cold. Your breath comes out in white puffs. There are no lights on in the building and the parking lot is empty. Half of the windows in the warehouse are broken and the remainder are boarded up. The trees have lost their leaves and they are spread in uneven clumps around the parking lot. Everything looks abandoned.

"Let's get out of here," you say. "Town's this way."

Seven years passed while you spent your last night in the warehouse. Your family is both overjoyed and frightened by your return. They have all aged. Your little brother is now older than you. Agent Smith is gone the next day, and she takes Night Breaker with her. You never see her again. The warehouse remains abandoned. Rumors of noise and lights coming from it in the middle of the night are frequent, but you don't go to look.

The End

"What do you want?" you ask the Brown Lady floating in front of you. You are still holding the broom in front of you. "Who are you?"

A chill wind from nowhere blasts you in the face as the ghost speaks to you. "RAYNHAM!" she says in a too-loud voice.

You drop the broom and cover your ears with your hands. "Wha-what?"

The Brown Lady comes right in front of your face. There is nowhere further to back away, so you stare into the darkness where her eyes should be. With one hand, she takes the veil away from her face and leans in. Besides her non-existent eyes, the rest of her looks fairly normal. She is almost young, with smooth white skin and a long, thin nose. Her lips have a brown color that matches her dress.

"RAYNHAM! RAYNHAM HALL! WE'RE LATE!" Though extremely loud, the voice sounds normal. An Englishwoman's voice, and she sounds angry.

"Whoa, hold on there, Ma'am," you say, dropping the broom and putting your hands up to ward her off.

She stops.

"I can't help if I don't know!" you try.

"My Lady, please," the Brown Lady says to you in a socially cold but normal voice. You stare into the dark pits of her empty eye sockets. There is nothing there but blackness. "I am a countess."

Go on to the next page.

"My Lady," you croak, "please, what do you want?"

"Lord Townshend will be very angry. He is most unpleasant when crossed. I am late. My brother, the Prime Minister, is coming for dinner. So is Lord Wharton. There is bound to be a quarrel...."

"Okay," you breathe, "slow down. You're not late for anything! In fact, we're early. I'm taking you there right now. Lord, um, Townshend won't be angry."

"You don't know him then," she tells you, turning and moving away from you. Warmth you didn't realize was lost comes back to you as she recedes. "But take me then to Raynham Hall! We can't be late!"

You follow the Brown Lady down the hall. The dim light makes her subtly creepy glow brighter.

"What about the stairs? Don't you have to stay with them?" you ask as she floats beside you as you walk down the hallway. The thought of running is the only real thought in your mind.

She turns to you with her empty eyes, "The stairs were fakes! Props for a mummers farce! Could not you tell? Come with me, we must meet the countess."

So saying, the brown lady stops in front of a non-descript metal door with heating pipes in insulation running around the jamb. Without anyone moving, the door opens by itself. The Brown Lady grabs your arm in a freezing grip and pulls you through the door.

Turn to the next page.

100

On the other side is a long stone hallway with roughly-cut and dressed walls. Lanterns with weak yellow oil lamps burning lazily within are spaced at long distances. You have to run to keep up with the ghost holding your arm in its freezing grip. Then you are pushed through another door. The Brown Lady stays behind as it shuts with a loud Clunk. "LOCKED UP! LOCKED UP! RAYNHAM HALL!"

Looking around you, your eyes are immediately drawn to the ornate bathtub set in the middle of the room. It is on a raised dais, with a white leather-covered bench next to it. Red liquid steams from the tub. The smell of hot blood assaults you.

"You'll need to excuse the countess," says a woman with a heavy Eastern European accent. "She is late. Nice of her to bring you here!" She is dressed in a bejeweled dress like those seen in old paintings of royalty. Sapphires and pearls cover much of her upper half and a blue dress flares out before dropping. She is young, and beautiful and clearly dead. "I am Countess Báthory. You may have heard of me!"

Turn to page 115.

102

"I'll get the replacement door," you tell Mr. Grady without much enthusiasm. Lugging around a big bucket of homemade poison doesn't sound fun, or safe.

"Great! I'll show you how you get there," he says, pulling a facility map out from his pocket. Even after two months, you haven't been in most of the buildings, and even those you've been in have lots of rooms you've left unexplored. You are still nervous after the moaning sink and the rats, but a little bit excited to see more of the unknown parts of the complex. "First go out into the loading area, then across the parking lot to the storage facility. Take this key," he says, removing a large, green key from his enormous key ring, "and remember to leave a note for the maintenance crew about the door! You don't want them thinking something broke in and stole it."

"Why aren't there security guards here?" you ask, having an opportunity to find out the answer to a question that has built up in your mind. "It seems like there should be, as there is a lot of expensive equipment around. There isn't even a guard at the parking gate—just the combo lock."

"Well, we've never had much trouble with people trying to break in here. Most people seem to avoid this place naturally," Grady says, looking straight into your eyes. "You should get going. We still need to get the night's work done."

Go on to the next page.

The summer night air is moist and the stars are covered by a thick layer of clouds. A faint hint of the moon, vague and dim, gives you a little light as you leave the yellowish glow from the loading area. None of the other buildings are lit up with activity tonight and you feel lonely as you walk through the dimness.

You turn on the flashlight on your phone again as you near the Dahmer Annex, but you only have 22% of the charge left, and the flashlight drains it quickly. You find the maintenance shop door and open it with the large green key. From the light of your phone and the glowing red EXIT sign in the far corner, you see all sorts of materials. Cans of paint, brushes, workbenches, and a large variety of bladed tools are strewn about. A series of scythes, from handheld to enormous, are lined up on a bench with a range of sharpening tools scattered around them. You make your way to the back of the shop and find another door with BUILDING SUPPLIES written on it. Hopefully this is where they keep the doors. Opening the door, you hear a shuffling noise in the blackness.

Turn to the next page.

"Anyone there?" you ask in a thin voice. Fumbling with the phone, you find the light switch and turn it on. Rows of windows, boards, latches, knobs, sills, and doors are stacked neatly in shelving. Moving forward a bit more confidently now that you have found what you are looking for, you head towards the particleboard doors.

Putting the phone away, you turn to your left and freeze. A little girl, maybe nine or ten years old, is looking up at you from the back of one of the shelves. Her legs are pulled up in her hands, and you can tell that she is trying to hide from you.

"Who are you? What are you doing here?" you ask her, trying to calm her, and yourself. The last thing you were expecting was a nine-year-old girl in jeans and a red sweater.

"You're not going to tell on me, are you?" she asks.

"Who are you?" you repeat, reaching out your hand. She backs away from you, but answers in a small voice.

"I'm Mary."

"It's okay, Mary, why are you here? Where are your parents?"

"They're dead," she says, closing her eyes and scrunching away as far as possible from you. "Don't tell on me!"

Turn to page 106.

"Tell on you for what?" you ask gently, leaning in towards her. You hold your hand back, not wanting to startle her again.

"Don't tell! I'm warning you!" she says, opening her eyes and leaning at you with a grimace on her face.

"Where did you come from? Why are you hiding in here?"

"I'm looking for the door out!"

"But this room doesn't have a door out. It's just a storage room. You have to go out through the workshop."

"Stupid silly!" she says. "I'm looking for the way OUT, not the way back IN! I need to find my Mama's ring!"

"What ring?"

"My Mama's ring, I just said that! Will you help me find it? It's here someplace and I need it!!" She looks like she is going to cry. "Please, help me find the ring!"

Go on to the next page.

"Look, it's like, 2:37 in the morning," you say, talking as you take your phone out of your pocket to check the time. "You should be at home... even if your parents...are dead...you should still be home. What's your phone number?"

"I don't know," Mary says, sulkily.

"Look," you say, tired by the whole night and exasperated by the girl, "I have to get this door back to the main building. Why don't you come with me, we'll find Mr. Grady and..."

"NO! NO! NO! NO!" she shouts, shaking in her little hiding spot. "You said you wouldn't tell!"

Turn to page 91.

108

Running as fast as you can in the dark forest, scrambling over boulders and falling on tree roots and branches, you get as far away from the evil exit door of the haunted warehouse. How could you have been so clueless? Everything was creepy from the first day. Why did you take the job? Why did you stay? You ask yourself these questions as you run to keep your mind from dwelling on the horror of your current situation.

WHAM!

You whack your head against a solid branch and twist your ankle in the process. Lying there in the dark forest, with your head throbbing and your ankle sending its own flares of pain, you feel very sorry for yourself.

After a moment, you pull your phone from your pocket. It isn't broken, although all that's left of the battery is 2%. Now is as good a time as any to use that last bit of juice. You turn on the flashlight. You inspect your ankle: it's not broken. Even though it hurts, this makes you feel better. Your head stops hurting quite so much, and you look around you.

Go on to the next page.

A skull in a rotting hoodie grins at you. Jerking away, you realize you are tangled up in the bones of the skeleton whose skull stares at you. That's when your phone completely dies, and everything goes black.

Turn to the next page.

110

"I'll come back! And I'll get my PAY THAT IS DUE!" you shout into the deep blackness.

Lifting yourself up, you continue on.

Thirsty and exhausted, you see the dim gray of dawn only gradually. But slowly the greens of the dark forest grow out of the blackness. You follow the rays of the weak, blocked sun. Finally you reach a road.

Picking a direction more towards the light, you walk on the side of the road. The forest thins a bit and you come to the backside of a brown sign.

On the front is a bunch of Japanese, you think, that you can't understand, but the other side is in English, a quote from Thoreau about the thought of dying without having lived.

I went to the woods because I wanted to live deliberately, to front only the essential facts of life and see if I could not learn what it had to teach and not, when I came to die, discover that I had not lived.

Go on to the next page.

A man and a woman dressed in park ranger or police uniforms drive up in a small car with lots of stripes and insignia. They pull over and offer you a ride. You must look like you need it.

They take you to a small brown building, hand you a cup of noodles (SO GOOD!) and a pamphlet. They give you solemn looks and speak to each other quietly in a foreign language.

The front is in Japanese, but the next page has a rough English translation.

Aokigahara Forest:
Please Consult the Police before you
Decide to Die! Lives are precious!
Do not end yours!
You will hurt the loved ones left behind.
Please enjoy the forest and the caves,
but do not end your life here!
If you find the remains of someone dead.
Report to station.

Turn to the next page.

There is a picture of a happy couple exploring a cave amidst the green, moss-covered forest. All you can think about is the skull staring at you. You have heard of this place and know where you are: you are in Japan, at the base of Mount Fuji, in the middle of the Suicide Forest. A place where people come to die. The people who rescued you think you came here on a mission to end your life—how could you possibly explain to them that you were actually just trying to complete your shift at your summer job, back in the United States? They would think you are crazy...maybe you are? You laugh and drink more of your soup.

The End

It is hard to make out anything with the smoke and the night blindness caused by the fire, but something, or someone, is moving out in the forest. *Just the wind,* you tell yourself, but you know that the wind has died.

Adding more fuel, you make a blazing hot fire that leaps high into the dark sky. Still, things move around in the dark. It is getting uncomfortably hot. You keep your jacket on even as you start to sweat. The sweat is from heat and nervousness combined into one hot, bad feeling.

A figure appears at the edge of visibility, between a jagged break in the rocks. It comes to you slowly, and you can tell that it is human, or was. Its head lolls to the side at a deathly angle, and a slack noose with a rope ascending into the sky circles its neck.

Slowly, it moves toward you. You back away, then turn to run. All you can hear is the fire and your heart as you spin. Coming from the other side of the fire are more figures with roped necks leading into the sky.

"No, no, no, no, NO! STOP! PLEASE!"

It does no good. Some dead do not want to be disturbed.

The End

You don't answer, you just stand there.

"Lady Townshend wanted to have you shut up and never let out, but I said, 'No!'"

"Th-thank you," you stammer.

"No need to thank me," she replies, smiling a chilling smile. "Locking you up and waiting for you to die, interning you, takes too long. We are late and Grady will notice if we tarry too long. No, we need to make sure you die much sooner than that. My bath is almost, but not quite full."

"Watch out!" you yell, pointing behind the countess, not knowing what else to do.

"I'm not dumb," the countess replies, "there is only one door."

As she says this, the door opens and two soldiers come through it. They grab your arms and hold you still.

"So, what do you choose? Heights or fire? It will be a test. You get to decide! Am I not gracious?"

"Let me go!"

"No, of course not!" the ghost replies. "You just get to make the choice on how you die!"

You decide to play along, if only to buy time to keep the ghost or her henchmen from attacking you immediately.

If you choose to be challenged by heights,
turn to page 26.

If you choose the test by fire, turn to page 68.

You are introduced to your teammates. Both are about your age.

"Hi, I'm Malik," says the boy, putting out his hand. "I'm the leader."

"Oh, and such an amazing leader you are!" the girl says sarcastically, coming over to meet you. "I'm Sarah."

"Nice to meet you both, I guess," you say shaking their hands. Malik's grip is firm but he doesn't try and crush your hand. Sarah's is equally firm. "Anybody have any idea what is going on?" you ask. The three of you are in a cabin in the middle of the woods. Hepburn and Padurii brought you there in an old Jeep. Even though the sun was shining, it still seemed like night. Things were very vague and misty and unless looked at directly, they shifted slightly. Hepburn took one of your arms, Padurii the other. Her fingers felt like talons and left red marks, while his fingers made your arm numb with white patches, like frostbite. They pushed you inside the cabin and drove off.

"No idea, but I would love to get out of this place, like now!" says Sarah as she tries to open one of the locked windows. "I knew I shouldn't have taken that housekeeping job at the Lizzie Borden House B&B, you know, 'forty-whacks from Lizzie's Axe'! But the money was too good. My friends said, 'Don't work there, that place is haunted,' but they paid twice what any other place did. I lay down to get a nap yesterday afternoon and I woke up with Mr. Hepburn and Ms. Padurii getting into my face!"

Go on to the next page.

"I was working as a busboy at the Stanley Hotel, you know, like *The Shining*?" adds Malik. "Everything was pretty normal. Except for yesterday. I whacked my head on a tray that was being pushed out in the kitchen. *WHAM!* right in the temple. My boss, who's pretty cool for a boss, said to lie down in his office. I fell asleep and then 'Skeletor' Hepburn and his buddy, the crone, came to take me here. How'd you end up here?"

"I didn't know I was working in a haunted place," you say, looking around the cabin. It is very rustic with a woodstove, roughhewn tables and chairs and three bunks built next to the walls. Water comes from a jug positioned above the sink. A bowl of fruit sits in the middle of the table. The door is locked from the outside and the windows are all shuttered. Light still filters into the room. "But sort of the same thing happened to me. One minute I was lying down after my boss locked me in a room, then next thing you know, creeper one and creeper two were there. Now I'm here."

"What are we supposed to do?" asks Malik.

"I thought you were the leader!" Sarah teases, but with an edge. "I think we just wait."

"I guess, but first I'm going to try and get out of here!"

After a couple of hours, the three of you give up on trying to break out, eat all of the fruit (bananas, apples, oranges, kiwis, and pomegranates!) and fall into a stupor halfway between consciousness and sleep. No light comes through the shuttered windows when a thick envelope is pushed under the door.

Turn to the next page.

"Team Exercise Number One," is written with precise calligraphy on the outside of the envelope. Malik picks it up and opens it. You and Sarah peer over his shoulder to read the letter. The inside is written like an invitation.

> *You have been selected to join*
> *in the 'Wild Hunt'*
> *(aka 'The Most Dangerous Game')*
> *Location: Crystal Lake*
> *Dress: Casual/Tactical*
> *Time: Midnight til Dawn*
> *Objective: Get Away!*
> *Survivors will be rewarded!*
> *Listen to your leader!*
> *(No RSVP required)*

"Rabbits! This is going to be awful!" Sarah says. You agree.

"What time is it?" you ask. "They took my phone and I don't have a watch."

Go on to the next page.

"No idea, same here," Malik says, and as he finishes, you hear the lock click and the front door swings outward. There is no one there. The night is dark, hot and still. "But my guess is that it is starting! Let's get out of here!"

The three of you creep out of the cabin, but you don't see anything or anyone nearby. Thick clouds obscure the moon most of the time, but occasionally a break gives some illumination. When the moonshine comes through you see that there are two well-worn paths, as well as the road, leading away from the cabin in different directions.

Far away, above the trees, you see red, blue and green lights swirling together. The sound of a distant hunting horn comes with the wind. Fear washes over you and you feel the need to run.

"I think we should split up," Malik says, turning to you and Sarah.

"Are you kidding me?" you reply, looking at him in disbelief. "That is stupid move number one in any horror movie!"

"Listen, I'm the leader," Malik says. "And I say that we split up. They can't chase us all at once this way. It's the only way we have a chance!"

"That's cute," Sarah says, her voice thin. "You think we have a chance! Do you even know what the Wild Hunt is? No one gets out alive!"

"I'm not just giving up! I'm taking the road. Don't follow me!" Malik says, running away from you two. He doesn't look back. The lights in the sky are getting closer, and the horn's braying is louder.

Turn to page 76.

"I'm sorry, Mary, but I need to make sure some-one responsible comes to get you," you say as gen-tly as you can, reaching out with your hand to take hers. "Mr. Grady won't hurt you. You'll see."

"Fool!" Mary spits out, her face turning ugly.

Before you can react, she lunges forward and bites you in the fleshy area between the thumb and forefinger. You can feel her teeth tearing into your hand, and the pain is overwhelming. Snatch-ing your bleeding hand away from her mouth and stumbling backwards, you watch as Mary runs to the door.

She stops and turns to face you. Your blood is all over her chin.

Go on to the next page.

"You should have helped me!" she screeches. "Now you'll never forget Bloody Mary!"

After four surgeries on your hand, you get most of the functionality back. Each time you see the scar you think of that night and how your world changed in one instant. There are no mirrors in your house and you avoid looking at windows as much as possible. Any time you look into something reflective, a scowling, bloody-faced image of Mary peeks at you from the edges. No one else can see her, but you do. Are you insane? You don't think so....but still.

The End

The Haunted Index

A partial explanation of the shiver-inducing
items catalogued in this book.

James Hepburn, 1534-1578, was the 4th Earl of Bothwell. Eight days
after the end of his second marriage, the Earl of Bothwell tricked Mary,
Queen of Scots, into marrying him and was accused of
murdering her friend and advisor Lord Darnley. Nation-
wide opposition to the marriage eventually forced him
to retreat to Denmark, where he was imprisoned in the
infamous Dragsholm Castle, where he was driven mad
after ten years chained to a pillar.

Ottis Toole, 1947-1996, was a serial murderer who drifted through the
Southwestern United States and was convicted of six counts of murder, lur-
ing the unsuspecting to their deaths with candy and keeping severed heads
as prizes. He died in his prison cell serving a term of life imprisonment.

Mr. Tory Perga's name comes from the concept of Purgatory, a term
which first appeared in Latin dating back to 1160. It is believed to be an
intermediate state reached after physical death, and in some literature, is a
physical place that can be visited.

Muma Padurii is believed to be the historical figure repre-
sented in the *Hansel and Gretel* story. She was a Romanian
folkloric figure whose name means "Mother of the Forest."
She was a guardian of trees, a thief who stole children, and
was responsible for burning down villagers' homes.

Winchester Mansion in San Jose, California was home of Sarah Winchester from 1884 until her death in 1922. Sarah maintained an enormous fortune after the death of her husband William Wirt Winchester,
a gun manufacturer. The mansion was built on the advice of a medium:

to house the spirits of people who had been killed by
her husband's rifles. The
madcap building that she
created without the help of
an architect had 160 rooms
and occupies nearly all of its
4.5 acre estate. To this day,
it is believed to be haunted by
many spirits.

`Bloody Mary` more properly, Mary I of England, 1516-1558, ruled England for only the last five years of her life but executed her opponents so ruthlessly that she became known as Bloody Mary to her detractors. She was the first queen regnant of England. Rumor has it that if you stand in the dark before a mirror and say her nickname three times, she will appear to you in the darkened mirror.

`Elizabeth Báthory`, The Countess, 1560-1614, is cited by the *Guinness World Records* as the most prolific female murderer. She lived a lavish lifetsyle in Csejte Castle in what is now Slovakia. Báthory issued invitations to local girls to come to the castle for etiquette lessons and to become maidservants, but murdered them diabolically instead. She ended her life imprisoned in Csejte Castle after a trial in which a witness said Báthory was responsible for the deaths of over 650 girls.

`Lady Dorothy Walpole`, 1686-1726, has become known in ghost-hunting circles as "The Brown Lady of Raynham Hall." She was unfaithful in life to her husband, Charles Townshend, who was known for his violent temper and punished her by locking her up in Raynham Hall, in Norfolk, Great Britain. She has haunted the premises to this day, and her ghostly presence is believed to have been photographed in 1933.

First published in Countrylife magazine, 1936

`Aokigahara` is a 14-square-mile forest at the base of Mount Fuji in Japan. Its unique terrain—a volcanic floor, an absence of wildlife, and very dense tree growth—makes it notably silent and also difficult to navigate, even with a map. A practice of abandoning aged victims in the forest to die was maintained until the late nineteenth century, and there is a belief that their angry spirits continue to populate the forest. It is now the infamous location of hundreds of suicides in present day.

`The Mary Celeste` is a merchant brigantine discovered on December 4, 1872 sailing with no crew off the Azores Islands. The last log entry was ten days prior. The cargo was undisturbed but the people who had been aboard were never seen or heard from again. A paranormal intervention was suspected as the cause of disappearance.

ABOUT THE ARTIST

Keith Newton began his art career in the theater as a set painter. Having talent and a strong desire to paint portraits, he moved to New York and studied fine art at the Art Students League. Keith has won numerous awards in art such as The Grumbacher Gold Medallion and Salmagundi Award for Pastel. He soon began illustrating and was hired by Walt Disney Feature Animation where he worked on such films as *Pocahontas* and *Mulan* as a background artist. Keith also designed color models for sculptures at Disney's Animal Kingdom and has animated commercials for Euro Disney. Today, Keith Newton freelances from his home and teaches entertainment illustration at the College for Creative Studies in Detroit. He is married and has two daughters.

ABOUT THE AUTHOR

After graduating from Williams College with a degree specialization in ancient history, **Anson Montgomery** spent ten years founding and working in technology-related companies, as well as working as a freelance journalist for financial and local publications. He is the author of ten books in the *Choose Your Own Adventure* series, including *Everest Adventure, Snowboard Racer, Moon Quest* and *Cyberhacker* as well as two volumes of *Choose Your Own Adventure: The Golden Path* and three titles for younger readers in the Dragonlarks series: *Dragon Day, Search for the Dragon Queen*, and *Your Grandparents are Zombies!*. Anson lives in Warren, Vermont with his wife, Rebecca, and his two daughters, Avery and Lila.

**For games, activities, and other fun stuff,
or to write to Anson Montgomery,
visit us online at CYOA.com**

THE LOST JEWELS OF NABOOTI

CHOOSE FROM 38 ENDINGS!

BY R. A. MONTGOMERY

MYSTERY OF THE MAYA

CHOOSE FROM 39 ENDINGS!

BY R. A. MONTGOMERY

HOUSE OF DANGER

CHOOSE FROM 20 ENDINGS!

BY R. A. MONTGOMERY

CHOOSE YOUR OWN ADVENTURE®
NIGHTMARE
EIGHTH GRADE
WITCH
CHOOSE FROM 28 ENDINGS!
BY C. E. SIMPSON